'n, Symeon

birtho

A SPECIAL BIRTHDAY

A SPECIAL BIRTHDAY

by SYMEON SHIMIN

McGraw-Hill Book Company
New York   St. Louis   San Francisco   Auckland   Düsseldorf
Johannesburg   Kuala Lumpur   London   Mexico   Montreal
New Delhi   Panama   Paris   São Paulo   Singapore   Sydney
Tokyo   Toronto

123456   LEBP   789876

Library of Congress Cataloging in Publication Data

Shimin, Symeon
  A special birthday.

  SUMMARY: A wordless picture book which reveals a young girl's birthday surprise.
  [1. Birthdays—Fiction. 2. Stories without words]
  I. Title.
PZ7.S5564Sp   [E]   76-14777
ISBN 0-07-056901-0   ISBN 0-07-056902-9 lib. bdg.

dedicated to Toni and Toby
whose birthdays were
celebrated in this fashion

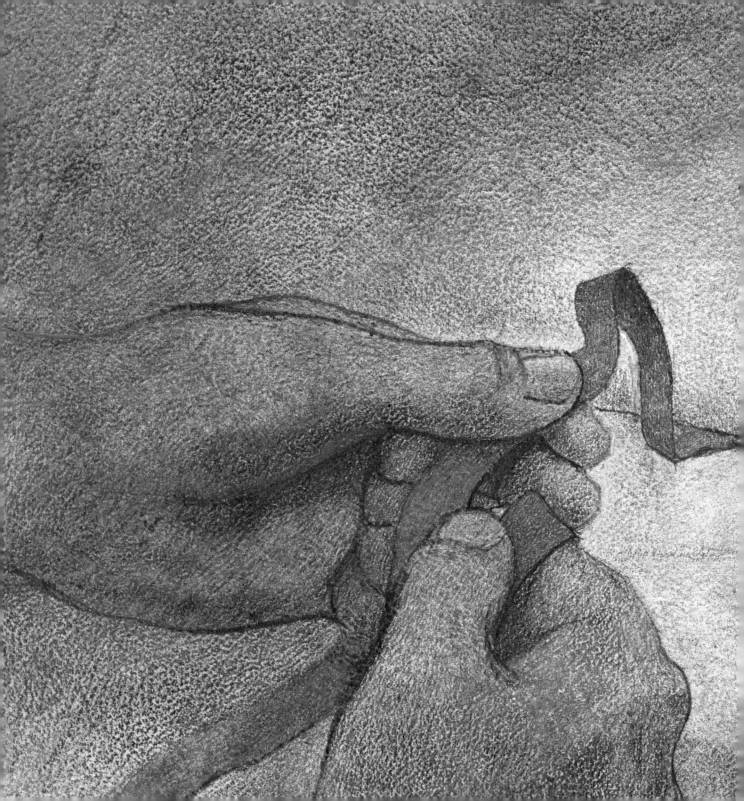

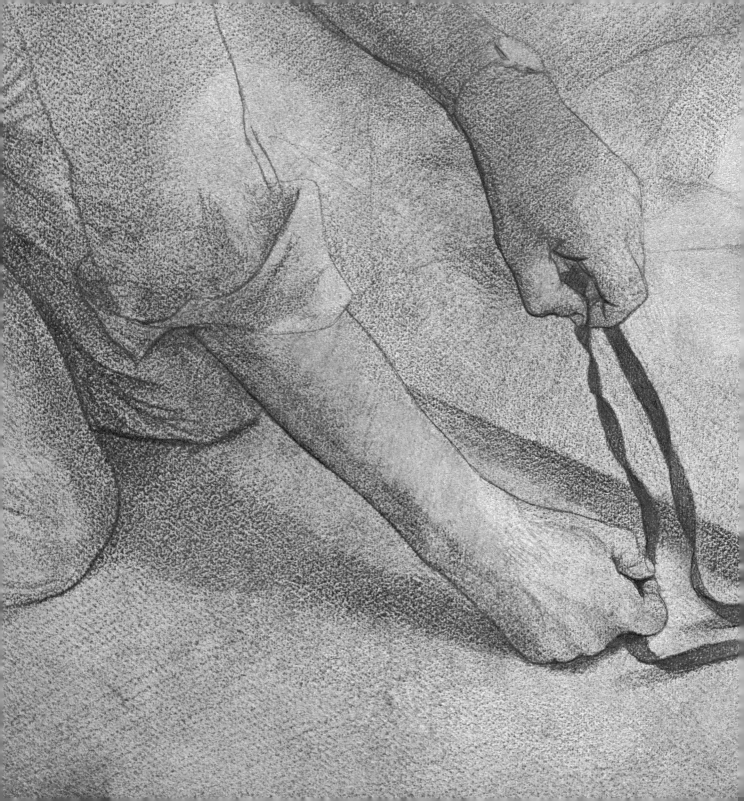

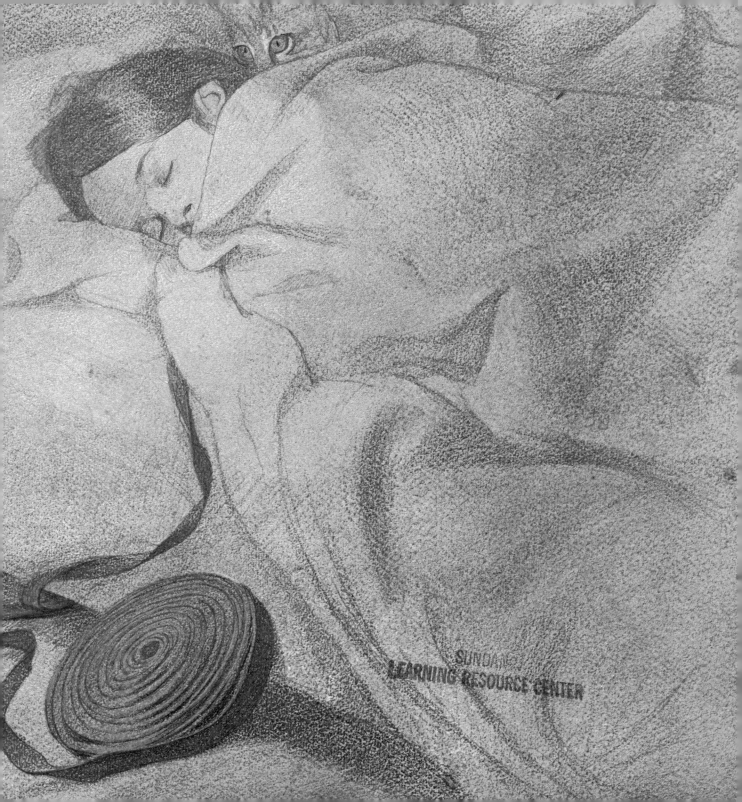

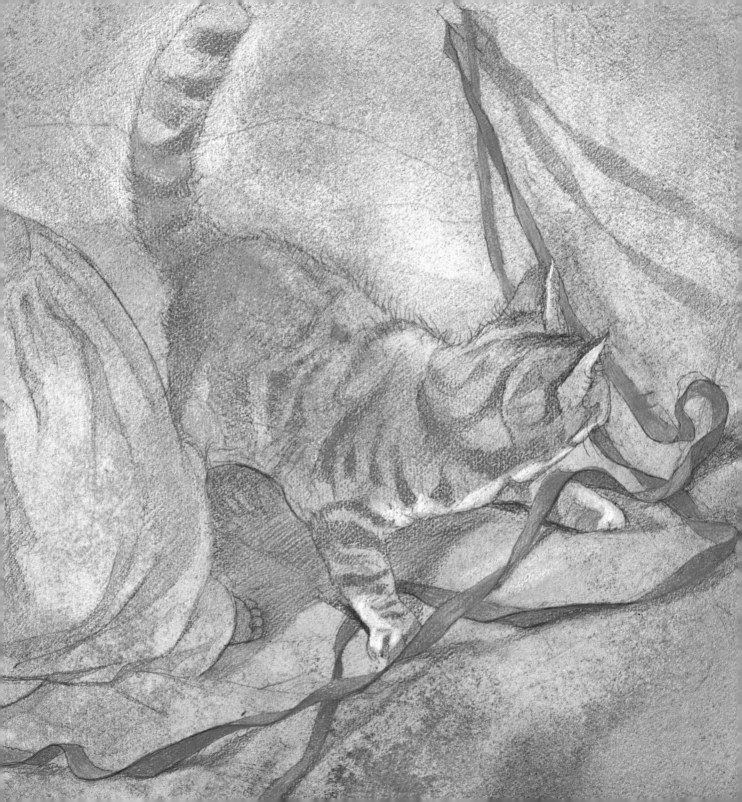

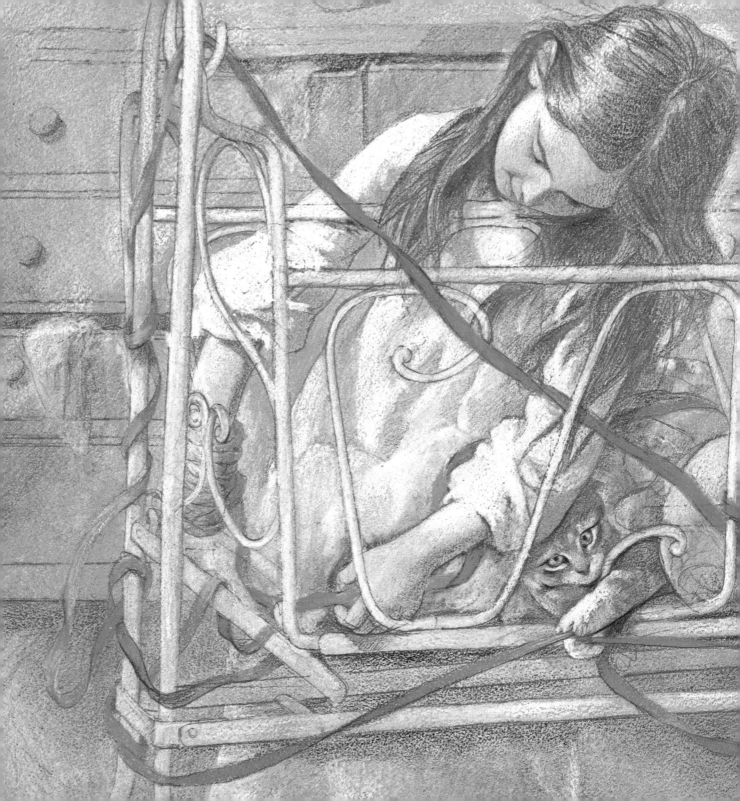

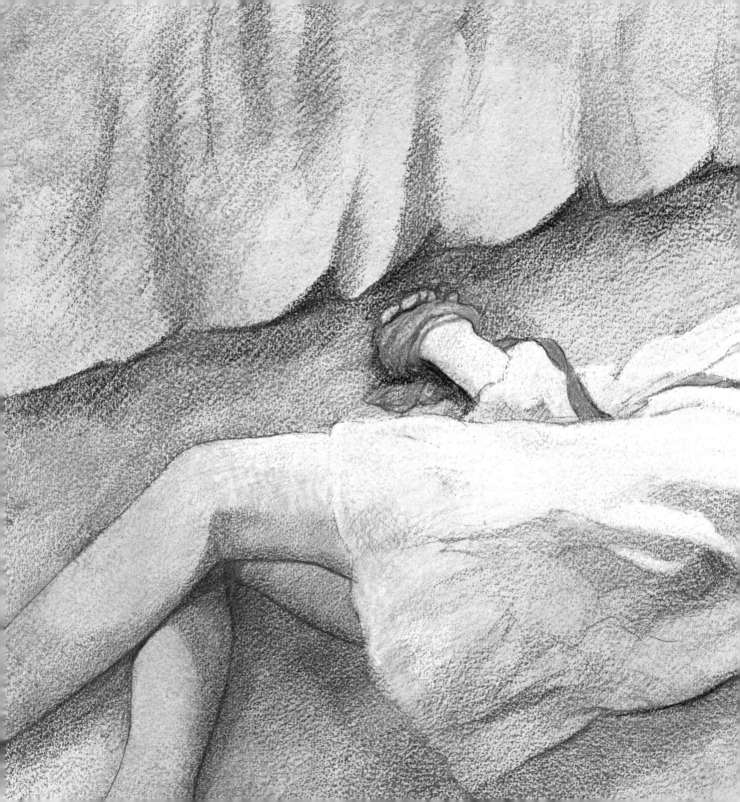

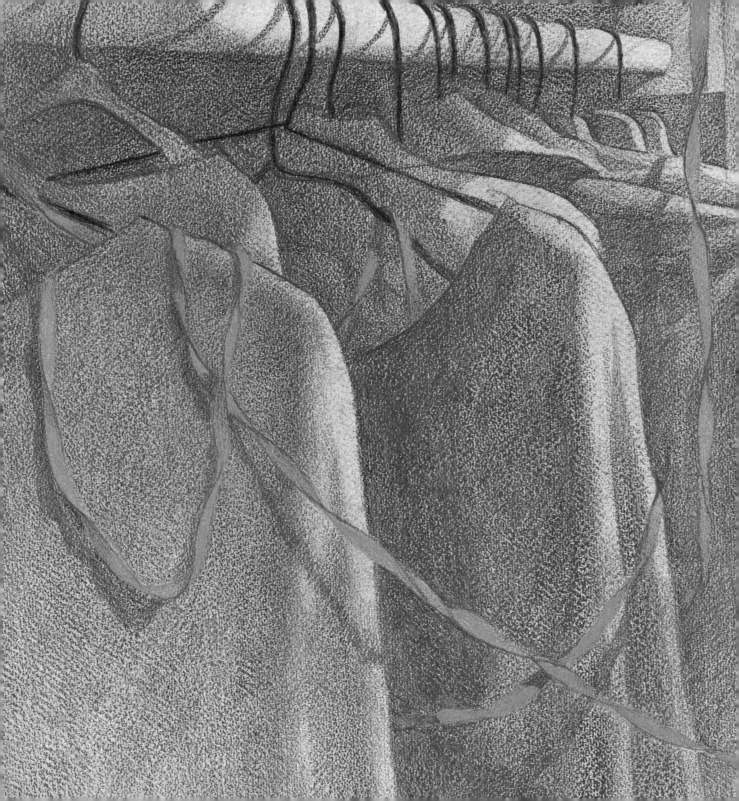